CARRIE'S STRENGTH

SONS OF HAVOC BOOK 1.5

CLAIRE SHAW

CONTENTS

Quote v
Blurb vii

Chapter 1 1
Chapter 2 7
Chapter 3 15
Chapter 4 28
Chapter 5 37
Chapter 6 49
Chapter 7 57
Chapter 8 65

Also By Claire Shaw 79
About the Author 81
Social media 83

Claire Shaw 2022

All Rights Reserved

The characters, places, and names are fiction and have been created by the author.

Any similarities to real life are coincidental.

This book may not be resold or given to others.

This book or portions of the book may not be reproduced in any form without written consent from the author.

This book is for 18+ only.

Contains adult themes, sexual violence, and adult language.

Cover Design – Dee Garcia – Black Widow Designs

Editor - Kim Lubbers - Knox Publishing

Formatting - E.C. Land - Knox Publishing

Proofreading - Alecia Rivers Goodman, Knox Publishing

❦ Created with Vellum

"You never know a woman's strength until you threaten her family. Never underestimate a fierce love."

Has Carrie overcome her fears, and can Joker help her on the continued path to recovery? Or will she fall into old habits?

When a new threat attacks the club, can a woman's fierce love for her family hold them together and fix what's been broken?

Can Carrie and Joker's unbreakable love be the bond that holds everyone together, or will they fall apart?

Will Carrie & Kate do what is needed to protect Havoc? Only time will tell.

Never underestimate what a woman will do to protect those she loves!

CHAPTER ONE

JOKER

Holding her close to me as she sleeps, I slowly stroke the hair out of her face. She looks so peaceful and beautiful, just resting in my arms with her head on my chest. I can feel the small puffs of breath from her pouty lips as she gently snores. The little noises are the sweetest thing.

I honestly still can't believe she's here with me, lying in my arms, in my life. A part of me, the part I didn't dare voice out loud, thought she was lost forever. I had hoped that one day I would find her, but as time went on, the hope got less and less. She was everything to me, and when she was taken from me before I even managed to see where the growing love could take us, I thought it was the end of me.

For the longest time, I felt like a vital part of me was missing. I didn't feel whole. Everything was in black and white.

The minute she walked back into my life; it was like a rainbow burst. Brightening my life. Who knew I was missing more, just her? Finding out I had a son felt like a power punch to the stomach. The air being forced from my body and leaving me gasping for breath. He's my image. My boy, Beau. Jesus, I have a son. Sometimes it still takes my breath away when he calls me Dad. Me, Joker, a dad for fuck's sake!

I struggle keeping houseplants alive, and now this actual small human being relies on me to keep him alive and raise him to be a valued member of society.

Thank fuck, Carrie is a natural at being a mom. God, she's amazing. So gentle and nurturing with him. It is like she was born for the role of mother.

Neither of us had brilliant childhoods. Carrie's mom was a queen bitch. She only cared about drugs and booze. My girl raised her younger brother, Johnny. My mom died when I was too young to know what a mom was and how it felt to have one. Our dads did the best they could. Reck got sent down, which left Carrie and Johnny in the care of the skank. Dad and I did what we could for them while Reck was inside. I wish we did more, as maybe if we had, she wouldn't have been taken by Child Protective Services and then in the hands of that sick monster.

Carrie shudders and whimpers in her sleep. Holding her closer, kissing her head, I whisper to her, "I've got you, babydoll. You're safe."

Fuck she still has nightmares and moments when she goes into her head. Who can blame her? She'd survived hell and managed to save herself like the badass my girl is.

Fuck I know I'm driving her mad, but I can't lose her again. I wouldn't survive it.

So, I struggle with her being out of my sight or not knowing where she is. I know she feels I'm crowding her and suffocating her, but I can't help myself.

Beau and I need her. I just can't let anything happen to her again.

She whimpers again in her sleep.

"It's okay, shhh. You're safe," I say in what I hope is a reassuring voice.

She settles for a second before she lets out a scream and jerks awake.

"Fuck, babydoll, I've got you," I tell her as I sit up and pull her into my body, wrapping my arms around her.

"Jason," she whimpers.

Her body is shaking, and I can feel the tears on my bare chest.

It breaks my heart to see her struggling like this. She's been going to therapy and working it all out. The nightmares are becoming less and less.

Fuck, it's only been just over a year since she escaped and found her way home.

"Jason," she says, her voice a little stronger.

"I'm here, babydoll."

"Make me forget," she says as her voice gets a little husky.

Her hand slowly strokes down my chest and beneath the sheet around my waist.

This is part of her recovery. Replacing the bad memories with good memories. Who am I to deny my girl?

Placing my fingers under her chin, lifting her face to mine as our lips meet. Kissing the sadness and pain away. Laying her back down on the bed, I kiss my way down her sexy as fuck body. Cupping her breasts in my hands as I take her nipple between my lips and suck.

Her back arches off the bed as my name leaves her mouth in a lust-ladened whisper.

Taking her nipple between my teeth, I nip it getting a moan from her. Fuck, the noises she makes when I touch her make me harder than steel.

Giving the other nipple the same treatment, I kiss each one and then keep trailing down her stomach and resting between her legs. Moving her thighs as wide as I can, I lick from the bottom to the top before sucking on her clit hard, causing her to cry out, and her body to shoot up from the bed.

Using my forearm to hold her still, I go to town on her and feast on her juicy pussy.

I can feel her getting close. Slowly I place one and then two fingers inside of her and stroke that sweet spot. My girl explodes with my name screaming from her lips as she crashes over the edge of her orgasm.

Not giving her the chance to move, I lean over her, kissing her as I push inside of her.

Fuck, holy Jesus Christ, this is heaven.

"Hold on, baby, this is going to be fast and hard. Fuck, you feel like home."

I start a punishing rhythm as my hands slide under her arms and hold onto her shoulders as I pound into her. She screams my name as she comes again.

"One more, babydoll, give me one more," I demand.

"No, I can't," she cries.

"Yes, you can. Give it to me. I can't hold on much longer," I say as I feel my balls start to tingle.

I move my hand between us and press on her clit.

"Jason, holy fuck," she cries as she comes again.

Feeling her pussy ripple around my cock causes me to join her as I roar out my orgasm.

Fuck, that was intense.

CHAPTER TWO

CARRIE

"Jason, holy fuck!" I cry as the most amazing orgasm takes hold of my whole body. Unable to stop the seizure-like tremors that rack my body. Jason's arms wrap around me, holding me to him as my body comes down from the high, he has just given me.

Snuggling my face into his neck, I plant a soft kiss on his chin.

"That was amazing," I say on a sigh as my whole body relaxes into his hold.

I swear being wrapped in his arms is my happy place. A place I feel safe, protected, and loved. But it is also a place where I feel confident and able to express how I truly feel without worry or stress. That's the thing about Jason, since I came crashing, literally crashing back into his life with the son he had no knowledge of, he's never held anything against me. I can be honest with him about how I'm feeling or coping. He listens and lets me get it all out without judgment. Which, in all honesty, is what I need. I hate that sometimes I freak out during sex, a movement or a word can send me back, and I get stuck in my head. Lost in the memories of what happened to me. I try to be the strong ol' lady he needs by his side. Losing my shit makes me feel weak. I hate feeling weak. Weakness is not something the Sons of Havoc deal with. The club is built on strength, loyalty, and trust.

I am loyal to the club. I trust every brother in the club, well, nearly every brother.

One of the brothers just sets my nerves on edge. Dog joined the club a few years after I left. I've noticed recently that a few of the boys I'm close to give him a wide berth. Joker and Tank seem to barely tolerate him, BJ ignores him, and my dad and Bull watch him like a hawk. He disappears at times with no word or reason. He's secretive, and my gut feeling warns me not to get close or be alone with him.

"You okay, babydoll?" Jason asks from beside me.

"Yeah, sorry, baby, just got lost in my head," I assure him.

I snuggle back down into his arms, resting my head on his chest. His fingers lazily trail down my arm.

"You have a session today, don't you?" he asks.

"Yeah, this afternoon," I confirm

"How are you feeling about therapy?"

"I know it's good for me, and it has really helped me work through how I'm feeling about everything that happened to me but . . ." I trail off, not really wanting to talk about it.

"But what?" he pushes.

"But we're now getting to the dark bits, before it's like we've skimmed over it, not really examined what happened, not only to me, but to Beau too. I don't think I can go into detail," I confess.

"Babydoll," he says, holding me closer, "she's a good therapist and has been good for you so far. She won't give you more than you can take. If you feel like it's too much, just tell her," he assures me.

"I know I'm being silly. But I can't help it. Part of me still feels guilty," I confess

Jason pulls away from me so he can look at my face.

"What do you have to feel guilty for?" he asks, confusion in his voice.

"I should have protected Beau more. I should have got Agnes to bring him to you long before I did. He could have been with you for years, and you wouldn't have missed out on so much," I say as a tear runs down my cheek.

"Fuck, babydoll. No, you did the best you could with the situation you found yourself in. Beau is fine, and we're together now. You can't live in the past, babe. We have to move forward with our lives. Otherwise, he wins," he says, holding me tight against him.

"I know, but sometimes when I watch you with Beau, the pain that you both missed out on so much time together hits me in the chest," I say as more tears fall.

"I think you really need to bring this up with Dr. Wood. Explain that this is how you feel," he advises.

"I will, babe. Can I ask you something?" I say.

"Carrie, you can ask me anything," he says with all seriousness.

"Will you come with me to the appointment, knowing you're outside waiting for me and close if I need you would help?" I say, hoping he can.

"Babydoll, I will always be there when you need me," he says, kissing my head.

Snuggling back into him, I start to drift off again.

Waking a short time later, I find the bed empty. Getting up and slipping some pajamas on and grabbing my robe, I make my way downstairs, following the noise and laughter.

Entering the kitchen, I find Jason cooking breakfast while Beau and Tank are sitting at the island playing some card game. I lean against the wall and watch them all together, my family. Jason has taken to being a father like it's the most natural thing in the world. The bond he now has with Beau is beautiful to watch. They are so alike; Beau is such a carbon copy of his dad. The brothers even got Beau his own kutte with prospect in training and next-gen patches. He wore it to bed that night, and we had a full fight the next morning to get him to take it off so he could go to school. I had to promise it would be in the car waiting for him when I picked him up.

His relationship with Tank has also blossomed. Tank is an amazing Uncle, but he is also that annoying

Uncle who buys him the presents you said no to. You know the ones, loud, messy, and completely inappropriate. But it is so worth it to see how close all three of them are. Beau has even started copying certain habits from both Jason and Tank. The three of them do all sorts of things together like we did as kids.

Beau notices me standing just inside the doorway.

"Momma look, Uncle Tank bought me Top Trumps and a new helmet for my bike. It's way cool," he shouts as he jumps off the stool, running into the living room.

Rolling my eyes, I make my way over to Jason, slipping my arms around his waist and kissing his shoulder.

Lifting his arm so I can duck under, I kiss his nipple.

"Cheeky," he grins.

"Something smells good," I say with a grin.

"Making you pancakes, babydoll," he replies

Oh my God, Jason's pancakes are amazing.

"Go sit down, and I'll bring them over," he says.

Making my way back over to the island, I grab a cup and make myself tea while he finishes my breakfast.

I'm just taking the first delicious mouthful of pancake when Beau comes stomping down the stairs all dressed in dark jeans, a black t-shirt, and his kutte. Fuck, he looks like a mini version of Jason.

Laughing around my mouthful as the helmet is still on his head.

"He take that off at any point?" I ask

"Yeah, once he tried to get his t-shirt over the top a few times and realized it wouldn't fit," Tank replied, causing me to choke on the pancake.

"Fuck babe, you okay?" Jason asks as he comes rushing over to me.

Swallowing the mouthful and washing it down with some tea, I laugh.

"Your freaking son, alright," I reply, still laughing.

Tank and Jason join in while Beau is standing there trying to put his biker boots on.

"I best help him," Tank says, still laughing.

Tank is keeping Beau for the rest of the day doing man stuff, as they put it. Jason and Tank bought an old, beat-up Harley. Together with Beau, they are working on it. Once Beau turns 18, they plan to give it to him. I swear when they ran the idea past me, I nearly cried. It is in the garage at the compound, and all the brothers have been helping Beau work on it. It really is such a warming sight, all these hard-ass bikers being so patient and kind with a little boy.

While they are out, Jason is coming with me to my appointment.

CHAPTER THREE

JOKER

"Babe, you ready?" I shout up the stairs.

Fuck she seems to be taking ages to get ready. Carrie is a low-maintenance type of woman. She could be ready for a night out in half an hour. A normal trip somewhere during the day, she's ready in 10 minutes. I know she is trying to delay leaving as she doesn't really want to go to her therapy session today. My girl is so strong and has handled everything that has happened to her with a strength that has amazed us all. But that being said, I know she needs a little push to let go and tell you how she's truly feeling. She keeps it all inside as she's putting everyone else's feelings first. I know Reck has tried to talk to her about how she came to be with him in the first place, but she shuts down. I know my girl, and she doesn't want to upset Reck. He already blames himself as he thinks if he hadn't got sent down, he would have been there for Carrie and Johnny. But Dr. Wood is right, we can't live in the past, and we have to move forward. The monster has no place in our lives now.

"Babe, seriously, if you're not down these stairs in 5 minutes, I am coming up to get you," I shout at her.

"Okay, Jesus. Keep your hair on. I'm coming," she calls back as she's racing down the stairs.

"Thank God," I mutter.

Heading for the car, I lock the house and get into the truck.

"You okay, babydoll?" I ask her. She looks nervous.

"Yeah, I'm okay, just want this over with," she says on a sigh.

Pulling up outside the doctor's office, I can feel the nerves coming off Carrie in waves.

"Babe, it will be okay. I'll be right outside in the waiting room if you need me," I assure her, squeezing her hand.

She gives me a small nod and gets out of the truck. She looks so unsure and scared. Fuck I hate seeing her like this. My girl is always so confident and sure of herself, but watching her as she slowly walks into the office, you would think she was walking to her death. I want to wrap her in my arms and hold her tight. The therapy sessions have been good for her. She's light and happy like she used to be. But the sessions also take it out of her, and she can be in a dark mood for a little bit after. Usually, time with Beau and me can bring her out of it. I know today is going to be hard on her.

Dr. Wood has been easy on her up to now, not pushing her too hard for her to really open up and let go of what happened to her. I knew there would come a day when she would need to examine it closer and really come to terms with what happened.

Checking in at the reception desk, we take a seat in the plush waiting room. Pulling her hand into my lap, I give it a reassuring squeeze while we wait.

Dr. Wood appears in the doorway not long after we arrive. She says goodbye to her current appointment and then smiles at Carrie and me.

"Carrie are you ready?" she asks.

Carrie nods her head and follows her through the doorway.

I sit in the waiting room, playing with my phone for what feels like hours when the door opens, and Dr. Wood pops her head out.

"Joker, can you join us, please?" she says, but she has a smile on her face easing my worry a little.

Walking into the office, I take a seat next to Carrie on the couch. She looks haunted. Resisting the urge to move her into my lap, I grab her hand again.

"Joker, I have asked you to join us as I feel it is important you know and understand how Carrie is feeling. But also, for you to understand what she has been through so you can help her work through it all," Dr. Wood says with a smile.

"So, Carrie, where do you feel the most comfortable starting? You understand we need to really look at what happened to you?" she continues.

"I don't really know where to start," Carrie replies in a small voice.

"Start from the beginning," Dr. Wood advises.

Carrie seems to be quiet for a few moments like she's gathering her thoughts and strength. Squeezing her a little, I slowly rub my thumb over the top of her hand, hoping she can take strength from me being here. She raises her eyes to look at me, and I can see the pain and fear in them. They punch me right in the chest.

"Babydoll, you are safe here, and I will not let anything hurt you again," I tell her.

Dr. Wood nods her head at me, confirming this is the right thing to say.

"It wasn't so bad to start with. He wasn't nasty to me, but he wasn't kind either. More indifferent. He ignored me most of the time like he barely tolerated me," Carrie explains.

"So, when did the behavior change toward you?" Dr. Wood prompts.

Carrie seems to take another minute to think.

"I'm not sure, to be honest. I noticed it more when my pregnancy started to show. Thinking about it, I really noticed it once my body started to change due to the pregnancy. My hips got wider, and I became curvier, plus my breasts were huge. It was around that time that Mom also noticed the change in him. She became angry with me, calling me a whore. Saying I was flirting and teasing him," she says.

I can't hide the shock on my face when she mentions her mom. Carrie had never mentioned her mom up until now. I store this information to discuss with her and the boys later. Reck is definitely going to want to know his ol' lady was involved.

"That must have been hard to hear from your own mother. How did that make you feel?" Dr. Wood asks.

"Hearing that from anyone is not going to make you feel great, but that wasn't the nastiest thing she called me. Mom never was going to win any awards for mother of the year, but it definitely got worse once he came into our lives. He supplied her with drugs," Carrie explains.

I really want her to tell us more. This is the first time she has mentioned anything about her time there or even how she came to be there. Reck and BJ have asked her a few times, but she clams up. I know it's going to be bad and it will be painful for her, but she needs to get it out so she can move forward.

"Is that how you came into contact with him?" Dr. Wood asks.

"Yes, Mom met him in a bar one night. Said he was her ticket to a better life, so I needed to do as I was told and not mess this up for her. She promised once we were stable, we would be able to have Johnny with us." Carrie stops and shakes her head.

"It was all a lie. She never wanted Johnny with us. She admitted it one night, when she was drunk, said we were better off without him as he was just like my dad. My dad is a good man. That got me a slap on the face when I told her so," Carrie says with tears in her eyes.

I squeeze her hand and rub my thumb over the top of her hand. I want her to continue, but I also don't want to push her too much.

"What happened between your mom and him?" Dr. Wood presses.

"She really thought he was this great guy. Great guys do not want anything to do with someone like my mom. She was a drunk, a drug user, and a whore. I knew I couldn't trust him. He had an evil glint in his eyes. I tried to stay out of their way as much as possible. But that became harder when we got evicted, and Mom moved us to live with him. I didn't want to go, but I couldn't live on the streets while pregnant. I needed to put Beau first."

I can't keep quiet any longer

"Babydoll, you did what you had to do to keep yourself and our son safe. Thank you for doing that," I tell her. I look at Dr. Wood to confirm I was okay to speak.

"Joker, you do not need permission to speak. Please feel free to ask Carrie questions. If she is comfortable answering, then she will tell you."

Nodding, I turn to Carrie.

"What happened to your mom, babydoll?" I ask.

"Her drug habit got worse, and she ended up owing him a lot of money. By that time, he was also sick of her crap. She basically sold me, and then he kicked her out. I never saw her again."

I sit there in shock. I knew her mom was more interested in the drugs than Carrie and Johnny, but to physically sell your own flesh and blood is beyond evil.

"I think that is enough for today. We can continue this next session. Carrie, you did brilliantly. How did it feel having Joker here?" Dr. Wood asks.

"I have no secrets from Joker and having him here gave me a little more strength to talk about everything. Maybe we can do the same next week? Joker joining us for the second half of the session?" Carrie asks.

"Of course, whichever you feel comfortable with, Carrie," Dr. Wood confirms.

"I will see you both next week," she says as she shows us out.

Carrie is quiet on the way home. Just staring out of the window as if in a world of her own.

Beau is still out with Tank for the rest of the day, and we're not due at the clubhouse to meet them for another few hours.

Pulling up into the driveway, I move round to Carrie's side and open the door, causing her to jump.

"Sorry, I didn't realize we were home," she says.

"I know, babydoll."

I take her hand and lead her into the garage. Passing her the helmet I bought her, with a candy skull and flowers on it.

She smiles as she knows what I have planned.

I grab my own helmet and climb on my bike, starting her up. I nod to Carrie, and she gets on behind me. I slowly pull forward and press the fob on my keys to close the garage door.

Once it's closed, we take off. Driving in no real direction, we head out through town and into the forest surrounding our little town.

After about an hour, I know she'll be starting to ache a little, so I pull off into the forest and stop at a picnic spot.

We grab a coffee for me and tea for her from the little van, sitting at one of the free picnic benches.

"Thank you for bringing me for a ride. The wind always helps me clear my head," she says.

"You don't need to thank me, babe. I feel the same. Wind therapy is good for the soul," I chuckle.

"Yeah, I love being on the back of your bike," she says with a smile.

"I love you being there too," I tell her.

We sit quietly for a while, just enjoying our drinks.

"Fancy a walk?" she asks.

"Yeah, why not," I reply as we make our way to the start of a short trail hand in hand.

We walk in silence, just listening to the birds sing to each other as we walk past.

"Are you happy?" she suddenly asks.

I stop and pull her arm, so she's facing me.

"Of course, I'm happy. What made you ask?"

"A lot has happened in a short space of time. We've focused on how I'm feeling and how it has all affected me, but no one has asked you. This has all affected you too. You went from being single to in a relationship with a child in the blink of an eye."

I love that after everything she has been through, she is still thinking of others and not just herself.

"I can admit it was a lot to take in at first, but Beau is amazing, and I love being his dad. I'm proud to call him my son. I'd been looking for you for so long, and now you're finally in my arms. I never want to let you go," I say as I pull her into my body and kiss her. I pour all my feelings into the kiss.

"I want to spend the rest of my life with you and be a family," I tell her.

"A family. Do you want more children?" she asks nervously.

I pull away from her a little, so I can look into her eyes.

"Are you trying to tell me something?" I ask.

"I'm not pregnant, Jason. I'm asking because if that is something you want, I'm not sure I can give it to you," she says sadly.

"How do you mean? Is it you don't want more children?" I ask, praying she says she wants more children with me.

I want nothing more than to see her round with my child. I missed out on everything with Beau and would love the chance to experience that with Carrie.

"Jason, no! I would love more children with you. You missed out with Beau, and to be honest, I missed out too. I never got the thrill of telling you and celebrating. I missed out on the love you would have shown and also the support. What I am saying is, after everything that has been done to me, can I even have more children?" The sadness and longing in her voice breaks me.

"Has the doctor said anything about that to make you think you can't have more children?" I ask.

"No, but they also didn't say I could either," she confirms.

"Babydoll, if you want to try for more children, then I am all for that. We can try for a little while, and if nothing happens, we can always get checked. If we can't have children, there is surrogacy and adoption. I will make sure your dreams come true," I promise her.

She wraps her arms around my waist and holds me tight. I wrap my arms around her, holding her to me. We stand like this for a little while.

Kissing the top of her head, I pull away.

"Come on, babe, we best get back."

CHAPTER FOUR

CARRIE

After our ride, I feel better. It felt good to get my feelings off my chest, and I should have known Jason would be supportive. He's amazing that way. Don't get me wrong, he has his moments when I want to strangle him, but he also has his good points.

Pulling up to the clubhouse, it seems a party is in full swing. I get off Jason's bike and wait for him to park. Once he's with me, we head into the clubhouse.

Tank and my dad, Reck, are at the bar as we walk in.

"Tank, where is Beau?" Not seeing him around anywhere, and I'm a little pissed he's here when there is a party going on. No little boy should see this.

"Don't panic, gorgeous. He's with Pip. He was helping her with something and wanted to spend the night," Tank tells me.

"That's fine, but next time let me know before you say yes," I scold him.

"Sorry, gorgeous, just thought you might need the break after today," he says with a smile.

I can never stay mad at Tank for long.

"Why after today?" my dad asks.

"Just had a therapy session today. All's good old man," I reassure him.

"Glad you're okay, baby girl," he replies, pulling me in for a hug.

We sit at the bar for a while, the guys talking as I'm people watching.

I notice Dog is sitting in the corner with a brooding look on his face. He's staring right at Wire, who is talking to BJ.

I nudge Tank, who is sitting next to me.

"What's going on there?" I ask.

Tank turns to look where I'm nodding.

"Fuck knows, gorgeous. Dog has had a bone between his teeth for a while now," Tank tells me.

"But what has Wire done?" I ask, being nosey.

"What do you mean?" Tank turns to face me.

"Are you blind? The look he is giving Wire is like he wants to kill him. I've noticed him looking at Wire like that a few times," I say.

"You always were so observant, gorgeous. I hadn't noticed," Tank says.

"Of course, you haven't. Men notice nothing," I laugh.

My laughter seems to catch Dog's attention, his eyes squint at me, and a snarl crosses his lips.

Fuck, what have I done to him? I feel Tank's hand on my leg.

"I saw it, gorgeous," he whispers in my ear.

Thank God, he did see it. It disappeared as quickly as it came, being replaced with the fakest smile I have ever seen.

"I'll bring it up with BJ and Bull. Just stay out of his way, gorgeous," Tank tells me.

"I have no problem staying out of his way. The man gives me the creeps. There is something familiar about him," I tell Tank.

"Familiar how?" he asks.

"I don't know. I've been trying to figure it out. Maybe it's because he creeps me out." I shrug it off.

"Let me know if you remember anything?" Tank asks, getting all serious.

"I will, I promise," I tell him.

Not thinking anymore of it, I go back to my drink.

I can feel Dog's eyes on me as I relax at the bar with Jason, Tank, and my dad.

"Just going to the ladies' room, game of pool when I'm back?" I ask Tank.

I love kicking his ass at pool. Making my way down the hall, I feel a hand on my arm, and I'm pushed face-first into the wall.

"I know what you are. You may have everyone fooled, but not me. I know what you are, and I will have my fill again," the voice threatens in my ear.

Before my brain can work out who the voice belongs to, something hard hits the back of my head, and it all goes black.

Waking a little bit later, I'm lying on the hallway floor. My head is pounding.

"Carrie," I hear my name shouted and look up to see Wrench running toward me.

"Fuck babe, what are you doing on the floor?" he asks as he kneels beside me.

"I need you to get Joker and Tank," I tell him.

I know I need them, but I also don't want Wrench to leave me alone either. As if knowing what I need, Wrench pulls his phone out and makes a call.

"Need you and Tank in the back hallway now," he says and ends the call.

"Can you sit up, honey?" he asks as he guides me up and back against the wall.

A few seconds later, we can hear the pounding of boots.

"Jesus Carrie, are you okay?" Jason asks as he reaches me.

Tank is behind him, looking just as worried.

"I'm fine. I lost my balance and hit my head. Can we maybe take this somewhere private so I can get cleaned up?" I ask as I can see a crowd has formed behind the guys.

"Yeah, sure, babydoll," Jason says as he helps me up.

Tank and Wrench follow us to our room at the clubhouse. Carefully sitting on the bed, Jason heads into the bathroom for the first aid kit.

"Carrie, do you want to tell us what's really going on?" Wrench asks.

"What do you mean?" Jason says, coming out of the bathroom looking confused.

"Seriously?" Wrench states with a surprised look on his face.

"Gorgeous, even I can tell you didn't fall and hit your head. You've had two beers at most," Tank says.

"No, I didn't fall and hit my head, but I didn't want to say anything in front of the audience we had in the hallway. I was going to the restroom when someone pushed me up against the wall and smashed something into the back of my head," I tell them.

I can feel the rage coming off all three of them in waves.

"And what else happened?" Jason asks.

That man knows me well.

"They may have whispered something to me, but not loud enough for me to recognize their voice." I honestly don't want to tell them what they said.

"You need to tell us what they said, gorgeous. I get the feeling you don't want to, but that means you need to," Tank says, gritting his teeth.

"Okay, but if I tell you, none of you can go off and act stupid," I pointedly tell them.

Jason barely looks like he is holding on.

"They said, 'I know what you are. You may have everyone fooled, but not me. I know what you are, and I will have my fill again,'" I tell them.

If I thought they were angry before, it is nothing compared to the look of pure rage on each of their faces now.

"Someone in our clubhouse right now said that shit to you," Wrench spits out while pulling his phone out and sending a message.

I don't have long to wonder who he messaged when there is a knock at the door and BJ, Bull, and my dad all enter.

I stay on the bed while they huddle near the door, talking in whispered voices and looking over at me every so often. Yeah, this shit is not going to work for me.

"Erm, you do all realize I'm in the room and know you're talking about me. That shit is just plain rude. Talk to me, and I will answer any questions, but do not discuss me like I am not in the room and cannot speak for myself," I tell them all.

The shocked look on all their faces would be comical if I wasn't so pissed.

"I'm sorry, sweetheart, we didn't mean to be rude. The boys were just filling me in on what happened. But you are right, we should have asked you. I will make sure we don't do that again," BJ tells me.

"Thank you, Prez. I appreciate it," I tell him honestly.

"I'm going to find out who hurt you in my clubhouse. This is a safe space, Carrie," BJ continues.

"You might want to start with Dog," I tell him.

"Dog?" BJ asks, confused.

"I noticed recently he's been acting strange, and when he thinks no one is looking, the evil looks he throws my way give me the creeps. Tank witnessed it earlier," I say.

BJ and Joker turn to look at Tank.

"I was going to mention it, but hadn't had a chance. I did see the look he gave her earlier tonight, and it was not friendly," Tank tells everyone.

"I've noticed him giving Wire the same look too," I tell them.

"Observant, sweetheart," BJ says with a grin.

"I like people watching," I say on a shrug.

"Okay, you notice anything else, let me know. Joker, I want you and Tank to make sure Dog is watched. I'm going to have a chat with Wire," BJ says as he leaves the room.

CHAPTER FIVE

JOKER

I'm angry, so angry I can feel the rage running through my body. The urge to hit someone or something is close to taking over. She was in the clubhouse, a place she should have been safe. A member of this club or a person we thought of as someone we could trust attacked my girl and said that vile shit to her.

As well as anger, I feel proud of how well Carrie has handled herself. She held her head high when she told us what had happened. Prez went to talk to Wire and called church.

I honestly do not want to let Carrie out of my sight right now.

"Babydoll, I have to get to church. Lock the door, and I'll have a prospect stand guard outside the door," I tell her.

"Babe, don't be silly. I'll lock the door, and I have my gun. No one is going to hurt me."

I know she is trying to reassure me, but it's not going to work.

"But someone did hurt you here, where you should have been safe. I'm not taking any chances with your safety," I say as I pull her into my arms and place a kiss on her forehead.

I feel her melt into me. I know she loves it when I kiss her head like this.

"That was a one-off, and you know it. I know you will find out what happened."

I love how much confidence she has in me and the boys to keep her safe.

"You know we will, baby. Lock the door behind me," I tell her as I leave the room.

I hover outside the door until I hear the lock and her chuckle from the other side.

"You can go now. It's locked," she shouts through the door.

"Smartass," I tell her back with a smile on my face.

Even when she's giving me sass, I love that girl. The sass makes me love her more.

Making my way into church, I'm the last to arrive, and everyone is already seated. I see Dog in his chair, looking bored. It's going to take a lot of effort on my part not to leap across the table and grab him by the throat to find out what his problem with my girl is.

I take my seat and look at Prez.

"Thank you for all coming on short notice. Unfortunately, there has been an incident tonight in the clubhouse. One of our own was attacked."

The room erupts as the brothers demand to know who and what happened. Taking a quick look at Dog, he looks a little more interested, but also a little nervous.

"Settle down, and I'll tell you," Prez shouts as he bangs the gavel to get everyone's attention.

Everyone settles down and takes their seats again.

"Tonight, Carrie was attacked. She's fine, just a little bump on the head. The fact is our Princess should have been safe to head to the bathroom alone in her own clubhouse." You can hear the anger in Prez's voice.

"Do we know what happened?" Cass asks.

"Not yet, but we will find out. I want you all to be on the lookout for anything strange, and until we get to the bottom of what happened, only family is welcome at the clubhouse. No strangers or hang arounds," Prez orders.

A few mumbles go around, but otherwise, everyone is on board. I knew the single brothers would be annoyed that they would need to take the random women they pull elsewhere to fuck, but tough shit as the safety of my woman comes before getting their dicks wet.

Prez dismisses church, but nods for Tank and me to remain. Once everyone is out, Reck closes the door.

"I spoke with Wire. Joker, did you know Carrie has been spending time with Wire, and he's been teaching her computers?" Prez asks.

"I knew he was showing her the basics and stuff," I tell him, a little confused as to where he's going with this.

"Turns out he's been showing her a little more than the basics," Prez says.

I'm trying to not lose my head, but what the Prez is hinting at doesn't sit right.

"My girl ain't no cheat, Prez," I tell him through my gritted teeth.

"Woah, wrong end of the stick, son," Prez says quickly. "What I meant was that it turns out our Princess has a natural talent for computers. Wire said she'd picked up the basics in a flash and wanted to learn more. He's been teaching her to be the next Wire. He seems to think she could be better than he is given the time and practice," Prez confirms.

I sit there staring at him dumbfounded.

"Fuck, really?" I ask shocked

"Yeah, shocked me too," Prez replies with a chuckle.

"Wire wants to keep teaching her and see how far she can go. I think it would be an asset to the club. She's smart. Our Princess sees things from a different point of view to us. The future of the club is looking brighter with her knowledge and skills."

Pride swells in my chest.

"Yeah, my girl is one hell of a woman. As long as she's not in any danger," I tell him.

"No danger, but you're acting like you have a say in this. You know as well as I do that Carrie is strong-minded and will do as she pleases whether you like it or not, Joker," he says with a chuckle.

I look to Tank to see him laughing away with Reck and Bull.

"Fuck, she's a handful, alright. I'll talk to her," I promise.

Leaving church, I head back to our room.

Walking through the door, I'm greeted by the barrel of my girl's Glock.

"Fuck Carrie, what the hell?" I yell.

"Oh, it's you," she shrugs like she didn't just have a gun pointed at me.

"Erm yeah, it's me. What the fuck? Why did you have a gun pointed at me, babydoll?" I ask, trying to get my heart to leave my throat.

"Someone tried the door handle not long ago, but didn't knock or call out to me. Figured it wasn't a good thing, so I had my Glock ready. You didn't announce it was you, so I was ready to defend myself," she says like she's giving me a grocery list.

Is this what our life has become? That it is so normal for her to have a gun in her hand and may need to use it to defend herself. I hope not, but she seems to be behaving like it's nothing.

I love that my girl is a badass, but this is not going to be our normal.

"Babydoll, you should have called me," I scold her.

"I would have, but in your rush to get to church, you left your phone here," she replies as she throws my phone at me. "And don't take that tone with me either, Joker," she shouts, causing me to stop dead.

Within a second, I'm across the room and have her pinned against the wall.

"Joker, really! I am Jason to you. Always have been and always will be. Yes, in the bar and with the brothers, you call me by my road name, but when it's just us, I am Jason, your man. This being ready to defend yourself will also stop. Yes, I want you to be able to defend yourself and Beau when I'm not around, but this will not be our normal. You're acting like it's nothing," I growl at her.

I know the second I have gone too far as her eyes glaze over, and she retreats inside herself.

"No, babydoll, don't you dare leave me. You know deep inside; I would never hurt you. Come back to me," I beg as her body goes limp in my arms. "Carrie, babydoll, please hear me. I love you with every inch of my soul. I will never hurt you." I whisper to her as I cradle her in my arms, just rocking her.

Dr. Wood had warned me that sometimes the least little thing could trigger her memory and cause her to be back in that house with the monster.

I've been so careful not to do anything that could trigger her. Not sure if it was something I said or pinning her against the wall that caused it. I've pinned her to the wall before, but that was during sex.

I sit on the floor with her in my lap for what feels like hours before she starts to stir.

"Carrie?" I ask quietly.

She shuffles herself off my lap, so she's sitting next to me, but not touching me.

"Babydoll, I am so fucking sorry. I would never hurt you," I beg her to believe me.

She's still not looking at me or acknowledging me.

"Carrie, please talk to me," I beg.

"I need a minute," she finally replies, her voice so quiet and meek.

"You take all the time you need," I tell her.

She gets up and heads for the bathroom, closing the door. My heart breaks when I hear the lock engage. I've fucked up so badly that she feels the need to lock the door.

I pull myself off the floor and sit on the edge of the bed, with my elbows resting on my legs and my head in my hands.

I can't bear the thought of losing her. We've been through so much and have come out the other side. This one small mistake cannot be the one to break us. At the thought of losing her and the pain I've caused her, I feel a tear slowly run down my cheek.

I'm not sure how long I sit there and cry. The next minute Carrie is crawling into my lap and burying her face in my neck. I wrap my arms around her and hold her to me. Relishing the feeling of her in my arms again. I have no clue whether this is a good or bad thing.

I feel her lips on my neck, kissing and nibbling at me as her hands run over my chest and down to my jeans. Her kisses move as she starts to straddle me, kissing me as if this is our last kiss. I pray to God it's not, but I ain't in no way in hell stopping her. My hands move from her hips to the bottom of the t-shirt she's wearing, pulling it up and off her. I lower my head and take her nipple in my mouth. This causes her head to go back, and a moan falls from her lips. Her hands move to my belt and jeans, I lift my hips so she can pull them off. My cock is already hard and it springs free.

Taking me in her hand, she lifts up and guides me home. It feels like heaven as she encases me inside her.

Moving to her other nipple, neither of us speak as she slowly starts to move up and down, grinding herself down on me. Fuck, this feels amazing. Both of us pour so much emotion into our touches and kisses. Our hands are everywhere as we touch every inch of each other. Holding her to me, I start moving at a fast pace, no longer able to take her slow movements, which are killing me.

"I love you," I chant as I pound into her, driving us both toward the edge and the release we both desperately need.

"I need you," she whispers back.

"I'm here, I've got you," I whisper back as I hold her tighter to me, feeling her clamp down on me as the first tremors of her orgasm push me over the edge and we come together calling out each other's names.

Knowing I'm not finished with her, I stand with her still in my arms and lay her on the bed. Hovering over her, I watch her face as I start to move again, slowly this time. Her eyes fly open, and she looks directly at me.

"You are my world, my reason for breathing. I would lay the world at your feet," I say as I slowly move in and out of her, our bodies joined together. "You are it for me. I couldn't carry on without you," I whisper.

"I love you," she whispers back.

I speed up a little causing her back to arch as my name falls from her lips.

I kiss her with everything I have in me as we both fall over the edge again.

Curling up beside her, I pull her into me, so her head is on my chest with my arms around her.

"I'm sorry I walked away from you. I needed space for a moment," she quietly says.

"Fuck babydoll, I am so sorry," I say back.

"Jason, you did nothing wrong, and I'm sorry my reason made you think that way. I trust you, and I know you wouldn't hurt me. Just sometimes, the stupidest of things sends me back," she says as her fingers trace the tattoos on my chest.

"Just know that I am always here for you. Please don't shut me out," I beg her.

"I promise to try and not shut you out. But sometimes I need to be alone to process where my head went and work through my thoughts."

"That's all I need," I tell her.

CHAPTER SIX

CARRIE

Things have settled down a little since my flashback. Dog is still acting strange, and I do everything I can to avoid him.

Jason and I are closer than ever. The sex that night was beyond sex. It was like we used our bodies to show our every emotion.

I've been spending more time with Wire. He's teaching me computers, hacking, and all about the dark web. This shit is so interesting. It's amazing the information you can find on the dark web and hacking into databases. Wire said I have a natural talent, and if I keep going, I have the potential to be better than him. I doubt I could be better than him. I watch the way his fingers fly across the keyboard without him even having to think about it. His eyes never leave the several screens he has, all with something different happening on each. Now that is skill, pure skill.

"You speak to Tank recently?" I ask Wire.

"Nah, he's not been around that much," he says, his eyes never leaving the screens, and his fingers don't stop.

"Yeah, I've not seen him much either. Think it has something to do with the girl he met at the range?" I try not to sound too interested.

"More than likely," he chuckles.

I follow his instructions as we hack into a security system. Soon the screens fill with the security feed for the gun range the club owns.

"Did we just hack our own system?" I ask, shocked.

"Yeah," he states as he zooms in on two people.

Looking at the scene, I realize it's Tank and a stunning woman. So, this is the reason I've seen less of my best friend.

A few clicks, and we take a clear shot of her face.

"Run it," Wire orders.

"What? Isn't that going a little far?" I ask nervously.

I don't feel right about running this woman through the system without Tank knowing.

"He knows. Seems he either has feelings for this chick or something in his gut is not sitting right," he informs me.

With a sigh, I start to run the face through the software Wire built. It runs the picture through the internet and government databases to see if it pops up anywhere.

The first few results are normal CCTV around town. It seems Wire has cameras set up all over town and at the club's businesses. When we start getting to government databases, the red flags start to pop up. No driver's license or record anywhere of her name, which Tank said was Pandora Jones.

However, one of the matches is for a Pandora, but not the surname Jones. This is for Pandora Chernov, the daughter of Nikoli Chernov. Nikoli is the head of the Russian Bratva here in Texas.

This cannot be good. Why is the Russian Mafia interested in the club? Russians usually keep tight control on their daughters. It seems Pandora is different.

"I'll let Tank and Prez know. Not a word of this to anyone else, Princess. This is the trust Prez is giving you by including you in club business like this," Wire tells me sternly as he leaves the room.

I lock his computers so no one else can see and head for the bar. Just before I reach the main room, Dog corners me.

"Sneaking around with Wire, Princess?" he spits at me.

"What, no! He's helping me brush up on my basic computer skills so I can get a job," I spit back as I try to move away from him.

"Sure, you are," he sneers at me, finally moving to let me pass.

Making my way quickly back into the common room, I see Tank at the bar.

"Hey, gorgeous," he says as I reach him, tucking me under his arm.

"Hey," I reply as I steal a mouthful of his beer.

"Get your own, beer thief," he chuckles.

Smiling, I make my way around the bar to get my own beer. A few of the guys notice me behind the bar, so they shout orders at me. Tempted to tell them to get their own, I start to make their drinks.

Turning to the other end of the bar, I see Dog standing there sneering at me.

"Beer," he demands.

I reach into the cooler and grab him a beer.

"A please wouldn't go amiss," I tell him as I slam the beer on the bar in front of him.

"Fucking whore should know her place," he mumbles as he walks away.

I stand there dumbfounded that he had the nerve to say that to me.

"You okay, Princess?" Angel asks me.

I spin around to see him sitting at the bar.

"Yeah, sorry didn't see you sitting there," I tell him.

"No worries, Princess. Was Dog giving you a hard time? He's been a moody fucker recently," Angel says with a shake of his head.

"All good," I lie.

I grab my own beer from the cooler and go back to sitting with Tank.

"Saw Dog at the bar, all okay?" he asks.

"Yeah, fine." I lie again.

I normally wouldn't lie to the brothers, but I have a feeling if I tell them what he's said to me today, that things would only get worse.

After a beer or so, I decide to head back to my room. I have a gut feeling shit is going to hit the fan soon in a very dramatic and deadly way.

Wire was nice enough to help me set up my own computer station in Joker and mine's room here at the clubhouse. That means I can practice whenever I want to. I also have an office set up at home too.

I decide to see what I can dig up on Pandora Chernov.

What I find is very intriguing, and I can totally see why Tank would be hooked on her. The woman is stunning, but also deadly.

The Princess of the Russian Bratva in Texas, she was not pampered like a normal Princess would be, hell no. This girl has trained with the best of the best. She is now the most lethal weapon the Bratva has, a hired hit-woman, but she also runs an organization called Phoenix. Phoenix is a group of highly trained women just as deadly as any man.

The more I research Pandora and Phoenix, the more I want to meet this woman.

Deciding to keep what I've found to myself, for now, I erase my searches like Wire showed me.

"Babe, you in here?" Jason calls.

"Yeah, I'm here," I call back.

"Thought you'd been sucked into the screen," he says as he wraps his arms around my middle.

"Aw, you feeling neglected," I chuckle.

"Fuck yeah, I am," he growls.

"Okay, baby, let's go to bed. Our little tiger will be home tomorrow." I grin at him.

"Yeah, babydoll, I've got a run tomorrow," he tells me.

"Be safe, baby," I tell him as I cup his cheek with my palm.

"Always. I will always come back to you," he replies as he rests his forehead against mine.

I know this life is dangerous, and every time our men leave on a run, there is no guarantee they will come back in one piece or come back at all. But this is the life we chose, and by choosing to love a biker, I chose to take the good with the bad.

CHAPTER SEVEN

JOKER

I kiss Carrie and Beau goodbye as we leave on the run. The run is a normal easy one, providing protection for the transport to the border, and then the other chapter will take over.

Simple, we have done this run thousands of times before without issue.

However, something feels off. My gut is telling me to take extra care this time. I nod to Tank, and he comes over to my bike.

"Got a bad feeling, bro. Keep your wits about you," I warn him.

"Yeah, Wrench and I got the same feeling," he replies.

"Wire is coming with us?" I ask, shocked as I watch Wire mount his bike.

"Yeah, BJ said he asked for the run as he needs to clear his head," Tank informs me.

"Okay, keep an eye on him," I say.

Wire never usually comes on a run like this as he's best kept close to a computer, in case we need him. Not saying he can't handle himself, because he can hold his own with the best of us. His skills with a computer are better than all of us, so if he's out, we're screwed.

Once we were all mounted up, we head off to meet the transport.

The hand-off goes to plan, and all is as it normally is. Nothing out of the ordinary. With the truck safely onto the next protection shift, we start the four-hour ride back to the compound. The closer we get to home, the worse the feeling in my gut gets.

Using the Bluetooth in our helmets, I group call Tank and Wrench.

"Brothers, I do not have a good feeling. Keep your eyes peeled," I warn.

"Same dude, feel as if shit is about to go sideways at any minute," Wrench says.

"Feel the same. Need to warn Wire and Dog too," Tank says.

I end the call and ring Wire.

"Watch your six, brother. We all got a bad feeling," I tell him.

"Feel the same too, I've warned Prez," Wire says.

"Good thinking."

"Gotta ring Dog," I say

"No, don't," his reply shocks me. "Just listen, you noticed how since we started making our way back, he's slowly fallen further and further behind?" Wire asks.

"Fuck, no, I hadn't. I was watching around me, not my brothers. Let me get Wrench and Tank on the call."

Adding them both to the call, I inform them what Wire just said.

"Yeah, I did notice. Been watching the fucker closely lately. Something ain't right," Wrench says.

Before anyone can reply, a black van appears from nowhere, and gunfire starts around us.

I watch as the van swerves Wire off the road.

Pulling my bike to a stop, I start to run toward him with my gun drawn when I feel burning in my shoulder, causing me to go down. My hand instantly goes to my arm, and I feel the wetness and stickiness of blood on my hand. Turning to Wire, I see three men in masks bundle him into the van and take off.

Turning to check on Tank and Wrench, I see Tank leaning over Wrench.

Getting up, I run over to them.

Tank has his hands-on Wrench's stomach, applying pressure.

"Stay with me, you fucker. You're not dying on my watch," I can hear him shouting.

Ripping my helmet off, I call Prez.

"Shit went down about six miles from the clubhouse. Wrench is hit bad, and I took one to the shoulder. They took Wire," I tell him.

"Hold on, brother, help is coming. Tank and Dog, okay?" he asks.

Looking around, I take a minute to see the bikes all laid out in the middle of the road.

"JOKER!" Prez shouts.

"Tank is fine. Dog is gone," I finally say.

"What do you mean gone, Joker?" Prez asks.

"As in the fucker isn't here. No bike. No Dog," I grit out.

"Okay, be there soon. Just hold on, brother," he says as he ends the call.

I look over to Tank, who is still applying pressure to Wrench's stomach.

I reach over and check his pulse. Finding one, I let out the breath I didn't realize I was holding.

"Keep the pressure on, he's got a pulse, and Prez is sending help," I tell Tank.

"We can't lose him," I can hear the fear in his voice.

"We won't. Just keep doing what you're doing." I try to reassure him as best I can.

It doesn't take long for the rest of the brothers and an ambulance to reach us.

I watch as the paramedics work on Wrench and get him loaded up into the ambulance.

"Keep the faith, brother," Prez says as I watch the ambulance speed away.

"Mount up and meet at the hospital," Prez orders.

We all rush to our bikes and speed off after the ambulance.

Walking into the emergency room, it is wall-to-wall leather. Prez goes off to see what he can find out about Wrench while a nurse takes me through to be stitched up.

Sitting in the curtained-off room while the doctor works on my shoulder, I hear her voice.

"I don't care, that is my man, and I'm going to see him." I can hear the fear and also the fire. The next second, the curtain is thrown back, and there stands my babydoll.

"Hey, babydoll," I say with a grin.

"Don't you fucking dare babydoll me," she fires back at me before she is in my arms and the tears start to fall.

"Hey now, I'm okay," I tell her as I try to soothe her with my one free arm.

"I was so scared when they told me shit had gone down and you were at the hospital," she says between hiccups.

"I'm okay, just a little scratch. Wrench is the one hurt more," I say without thinking.

"Do you honestly think that makes it better? I love all of you, so when one of you gets hurt, I still hurt and worry. Plus, it is not a scratch. You were fucking shot!" Her voice trailing off into an angry whisper yell.

Wow, my baby girl is fired up tonight.

"I know, baby, and I'm sorry." I pull her to me as the doctor finishes my stitches.

Wrapping me up, he gives the care instructions to Carrie, confirming it was just a graze and the bullet missed me. From the look on Carrie's face, she's not impressed with how unconcerned the doctor seems to be.

Joining the rest of the brothers in the waiting room, we wait to hear how Wrench is.

"Jason, as much as I want to wait here with you, Beau needs me. He was around when everything happened, so I want to make sure he's okay," Carrie says from beside me.

"Yeah, okay, two of the prospects will take you back."

Nodding, she kisses me, stops to give Tank a hug, and has a quick chat with Prez before she leaves.

The waiting continues.

I replay everything that happened over and over in my head, trying to figure out what we missed.

I didn't notice the van or Dog acting strange.

Nodding to Tank, he comes and joins me.

"How are you feeling, brother?" he asks.

"Like shit, I keep replaying the whole day over and over. Trying to remember if we missed anything."

"Same. I can't think of a single thing I noticed. Wrench will be fine, and we will get Wire back," Tank says with conviction in his voice.

"Anyone else taken, then yeah I would agree. But fuck, Wire was our secret weapon. Now we have no Wire to do his computer shit and find him." I hate saying the words out loud.

"Have a little faith, brother," Tank says.

CHAPTER EIGHT

CARRIE

Sitting in the common room with Beau and Kate, I hear the yelling and the brothers all jumping into action.

I jump up and turn to Kate.

"Get Beau out of here," I say.

Nodding, she scoops him up, and I hear her say something about watching a film to him.

I can see in his eyes that he knows something is wrong.

I look around as the brothers all seem to be preparing to leave. From the hall, I hear Prez yell

Joker's name. My heart drops. Fuck no. Please, God, no. Not Jason.

Making my way down the hall, I find Prez leaving his office.

"Don't lie, just give it to me straight," I tell him.

"Shit's gone down; Joker is fine, but Wrench has been shot. Wire and Dog are missing. Tank is fine too," he tells me.

Nodding my head, I can breathe a little easier knowing he's okay.

"What can I do?" I ask

Smiling, Prez pulls me in for a hug and kisses the top of my head.

"Perfect ol' lady," he murmurs.

"I'm going to them now. I'll let you know when we're on our way to the hospital. The prospects will bring you to meet us," he says as he takes off down the hall.

Needing to keep busy, I go make sure Beau is okay.

I find him in the cinema/family room with Kate watching kids TV.

"All okay?" Kate asks at the same time as Beau.

"Dad, okay?"

Smiling at the pair of them, I join them on the sofa. I love how close they have become. Beau truly loves his Aunty Kate.

"Yeah, your dad's fine. Everything is fine," I tell him as I pull him into my lap.

Giving Kate a look, I know she'll understand. She nods and then asks.

"Who wants a hot chocolate with marshmallows?"

"Me, me," Beau replies, jumping up and down.

Chuckling, Kate gets up to go make them.

"Carrie, can you give me a hand," she asks

"Of course," I nod, following her to the kitchen.

Once we're out of earshot, she turns to me.

"What the fuck is going down?" she asks.

"As far as I know, the run didn't end so well. Wrench has been shot. Joker and Tank are fine, but Wire and Dog are missing."

"Don't you find that strange?" she says with a confused look on her face.

"How do you mean?" I ask

"Dog has been acting really strange recently, and I've caught him trying to get into Wire's room a few times."

Well, this is news to me. I agree Dog has been acting shady as fuck recently.

"Yeah, I agree he's been acting shady, but I didn't know he tried to get into Wire's room," I tell her.

Finishing the hot chocolates, I run over everything and all the weird things that have happened. Just trying to make sense of it all.

Joining Beau back on the sofa, we're halfway through the film when my phone goes off.

"Prez," I answer.

"Everything is okay. Prospects are coming to pick you up," he says and ends the call.

Short and sweet as always.

"Buddy, I need to pop out for a little bit. Are you okay here with Aunt Kate?" I ask.

"Yeah, Mom, I'll be fine. Tell Dad and Uncle Tank I love them. Wire and Wrench too, but not Dog."

Raising my eyebrow at him, I ask.

"Why not Dog?"

"Dog is nasty, and he says mean things about you."

What the actual fuck.

"Beau, buddy. Has Dog ever hurt you?"

"Not really, he's rough sometimes, but he says mean things about you."

Pulling my son into my arms, I hold him close.

"He will never go near you again," I promise.

Kissing his head, I look to Kate and see the rage on her face.

Nodding to show I agree, I head out to meet the prospects.

Getting to the hospital, I see Tank and Prez in the waiting room along with everyone else. Looking around, I can't see Jason.

"He's getting fixed up," Tank tells me.

Stopping dead in my tracks, I turn to face him.

"What do you mean, getting fixed up?" I ask, trying not to freak out.

"He was grazed, and the doc is fixing him up," he replies as if it's nothing

"You mean to tell me my man was shot, and no one fucking bothered to tell me?" By this point, I know I'm yelling.

"Calm down, gorgeous, it's a scratch. He's fine."

Before he can say anything else, I'm storming down the corridor toward the treatment rooms.

Checking the board as I pass, I see he's in cubicle 4.

"Carrie, calm down. He'll be out in a minute," Tank tries to say behind me.

Spinning around, I punch him full force in the stomach, causing him to double over.

"I don't care, that is my man, and I'm going to see him," I yell at him.

Storming toward cubicle 4, I throw the curtain back, and there sits my man.

"Hey, Babydoll," he says with a grin.

"Don't you fucking dare babydoll me," I fire back at him before I throw myself at him and the tears start to fall.

"Hey now, I'm okay," he tells me as he tries to soothe me.

"I was so scared when they told me shit had gone down and you were at the hospital," I say between hiccups.

"I'm okay, just a little scratch. Wrench is the one hurt more," he says.

Seriously, fucking idiot.

"Do you honestly think that makes it better? I love all of you, so when one of you gets hurt, I still hurt and worry. Plus, it is not a scratch. You were fucking shot!" My voice trails off into an angry whisper yell.

"I know, baby, and I'm sorry," he says as the doctor finishes stitching him up.

Once we're back in the waiting room, I can't help thinking about who is going to find Wire. He's the computer genius.

Moving to get a drink, I hear Prez on his phone.

"No, we have no clue who's taken them. This is a fucking shit storm."

Holy fuck!

If they don't know who is behind this, then how are they going to get Wire back? I know Dog is missing too, but something tells me he's missing for a whole other reason.

Making my way back to Jason, I sit for a while longer. A plan starts to form in my head. I am sick of sitting back and watching shit happen to the people I love.

I tell Jason I need to get back to Beau. He agrees, and the prospects take me back to the clubhouse.

Once back, I find Kate in the family room.

"Beau's in bed," she tells me.

"Good, because we have shit to do if you're in?" I say.

"Oh, hell yes, I am in. Hate sitting around waiting for the men to deal with business."

God, I love this girl.

Heading for my room, I start a search for Wire's phone and run everything I can find on Dog.

"What's the plan, girl?" Kate asks.

"My plan is to find Wire, and I know the answer lies with Dog. But I think we're going to need help."

I know this is going to piss the brothers off, but at the moment, I could care less.

Picking up my phone, I dial the number I have hidden.

"Yes," comes the feminine voice

"You don't know me, but I have a feeling you'll want to help me," I tell her.

She laughs this manic cackle.

"What makes you so sure I'm going to want to help you? I don't even know you," she replies

"If Tank means anything to you, you'll help me," I tell her.

"Tank," she says, and now I know I have her attention.

"Yes, I'm Gorgeous, and I need your help saving my family," I say honestly.

The line is quiet for what feels like a lifetime.

"I'm in," she finally replies.

An evil smirk spreads across my face.

"Good, because we're about to fuck shit up!"

The End.

*This dedication is a little different. The novella was
originally released in the Twisted Steel First Edition.
It was an absolute honor and pleasure to work alongside
some amazing authors who have not only inspired me, but
have also been my idols!
As a new author, they didn't get frustrated or annoyed
when I asked loads of stupid questions . . . Yes, somewhere
completely stupid questions!!!
They helped guide me, gave me priceless advice, and
helped me learn more about myself as an author.
Thank you, Elizabeth Knox (Jessica Evans), Addison Jane,*

Amy Davies, Erin Osborne, Chelle C. Craze, E.C. Land, Scarlett Black, Rae B. Lake, Nia Farrell, & Dani Rene. The story came about from frustration on my part. I am an avid reader, and MC is my favorite genre. However, that being said, women in MC books tend to be helpless and need to be saved, babied, and protected by the big strong bikers.

I know this is not for all books and authors.
I love a strong woman, one that stands up for not only herself, but those she loves.

I was raised by a Mom who can take grown bikers to their knees with a look and a few words, yet you look at her, and she's so elegant, kind, and caring.

I am also lucky enough to have three crazy Aunties who are all so strong in their own ways.

All four of them were raised by my Granny Hepple, who was an amazing woman. No one messed with Granny Hepple. If you did, you would know about it.

But what I remember most about growing up was the feeling of family and how we can call each other (the aunties do not mince words and call it exactly as they see it), but no one else could.

We love, support, and protect each other no matter what life throws at us.

My amazing girls, who smile no matter what life throws at them. My life is better, because you are all in it!

Helen, Kate, & Tracy - you are my sisters for life!
A Woman's strength should be celebrated!
This book celebrates the strong & amazing women in my life!

ALSO BY CLAIRE SHAW

Sons Of Havoc

Texas Chapter Series

Joker

Havoc Novella

Tank

Havoc Christmas

Wire – Coming soon

Sons of Havoc

Phoenix Chapter

Bishop – coming soon

ABOUT THE AUTHOR

USA Today Bestselling Author Claire is a Yorkshire girl through and through. She is married and has two fur babies. Claire is a bit of gypsy, loving to roam and have fun, and always up for an adventure.

With her eclectic taste in music, from Country to Old Skool R&B to Classic Rock, Claire started writing after being encouraged by some of her favorite authors and friends. Being so close to her family and being a daddy's girl, she started to write what she knew, which is MC Romance.

With her dad being in a club when she was younger, she has been surrounded by bikers most of her life.

Using the influence of her momma and crazy aunties, Claire loves to write about strong women who stand up and take no rubbish. So, she created the world of Sons of Havoc MC and their badass women.

Social Links

Website
Facebook
Facebook Group
Instagram
Goodreads

Printed in Great Britain
by Amazon